To

....

HAPPY EASTER

Love from,

....

The Easter Egg Hunt in INDIANA

Written by Laura Baker   Illustrated by Jo Parry

HOMETOWN WORLD

It's Easter time in Indiana!
Bunny bounces out of bed,
feeling grateful for this day,
and everything ahead.

Mommy Bunny smiles and says:
"Springtime's in the air.
Time to search for eggs and love.
We'll find them everywhere!"

Will YOU help them look too?

Just outside Evansville,
they search up, down... everywhere!
Hopping along, paw in paw,
Bunny says: "How about over there?"

Playful lambs call over,
with a kind and happy bleat.
"Happy Easter, woolly friends—
Look! Our first Easter treat!"

HOOSIER
FARM

With one egg in the basket,
the bunnies stop beside a brook.
Bloomington, Greencastle, or Carmel?
Oh, which way should they look?

Ducklings splash, quack, and wave.
"Maybe try along the water!"
Bunny's thankful for the help:
"Now, I'm a real egg spotter!"

Two eggs in the basket,
the pace is picking up!
And when the bunnies reach Terre Haute,
they're greeted with a "Cluck!"

"We can't stay long," Little Bunny says,
"although visiting is so sweet.
We have lots of eggs to find—
is that one underneath?"

On the path to Lafayette,
they stop to see the bees.
Perhaps they'll find some more eggs
hiding in the leaves!

CONNER PRAIRIE

HOOSIER FARM

They stop and smell the flowers
in the field around the hive.
Counting: "One, two, three... there's four!
Now on to find egg five!"

The bunnies pause in South Bend,
as a rainbow fills the sky.
Mommy watches fondly
while Bunny looks nearby.

They cuddle and give thanks
for the blessings of the day.
Then clever Bunny spots it—
"A pink one now, hooray!"

Off to a market in Fort Wayne,
they meet lots of friendly faces.
The bunnies search and peep for eggs
through all their favorite places.

Peony Farm

Indiana Treats

A park in Muncie has a spot to take a seat.
Even eggs-pert treasure hunters must stop to rest their feet.

"Have you seen any eggs?" Bunny asks a family.
"Why yes," smiles Raccoon. "Look up there in that tree!"

Happy Easter

In puddles by French Lick, Bunny splashes all around.
"Over here," calls Mommy. "Another egg to be found!"

"Let's search for more!" cries Bunny,
and then they dash away...

...to Noblesville,
where more friends want to play!

Bright-eyed pups play hide-and-seek
in the farmer's field.
What's that pup sniffing there?
A new egg is revealed!

The sun in Indianapolis is setting for the day,
and Little Bunny takes this chance to hop about and play.
With an Easter basket full, and a joyful, grateful heart,
Bunny's ready to be home—right back to the start.

Back through Noblesville-woof, woof, jump.

Back through French Lick-oink, oink, grunt.

Back past Muncie—crunch, crunch, yum.

Back past Fort Wayne—the busy day is done.

Back through South Bend–neigh, neigh… "Whee!"

Back past Terre Haute–cheep, cheep… "Follow me!"

Back past the brook–quack, quack... "Come!"

Back to Evansville–baa, baa... "Run!"

Back home at Bunny Tree, they feast and count their haul.
"One, two, three, four, five, six, seven, eight, nine..."

Did YOU find them all?

Little Bunny says: "While counting all our eggs,
let's count our blessings, too.
Friends, family, fun...
and an Easter spent with you!"

As the stars shine down on Indiana,
Bunny snuggles into bed.
"Hoppy Easter," whispers Mommy.
"I love you, sleepyhead."

Written by Laura Baker
Illustrated by Jo Parry
Designed by Ryan Dunn

Copyright © Bidu Bidu Books Ltd. 2023

Published by Hometown World,
an imprint of Sourcebooks Kids
P.O. Box 4410, Naperville, Illinois 60567-4410
(630) 961-3900
hometownworld.com
sourcebookskids.com

Source of Production: 1010 Asia Limited,
North Point, Hong Kong, China
Date of Production: July 2022
Run Number: 5026279
Printed and bound in China (OGP)
10 9 8 7 6 5 4 3 2 1